Karma the crocodile

ANGRY CLOUDS

Created and Written by

Frank Navratil

Karma Kyle the Crocodile
Angry Clouds

KARMA KYLE
PRODUCTIONS

First Edition
Published by Karma Kyle Productions
Frank Navratil
Purkynova 1246/9
Ricany, Czech Republic

Visit our web site at:
www.karmakyle.com

ISBN 978-80-88022-12-1

"Holding on to anger is like grasping a hot coal with the intent of throwing it at someone else; you are the one who gets burned."
The Buddha

To Jana:

Your love always helps me ward away my occasional angry clouds.

Karma Kyle woke up one day,
on the wrong side of the bed.
He got into an angry mood,
when he fell and hit his head.

"Ouch, that really hurt," he said.
"Today is not my day."
He looked outside the window.
Angry Clouds had come his way.

"Oh no!" said Karma Kyle.
"I don't want them here with me.
Angry clouds just want to stay.
They will not let me be."

They change the world to black and grey,
wherever you may look.
They even took some colors
from the pages of this book.

Then things got out of hand,
and they turned out for the worst.
He pushed his sister Kacy,
to get in the bathroom first.

"Mama Croc! He pushed me!"
Kacy cried and tried to talk.
His mother sent poor Karma Kyle
to talk to Papa Croc.

"What is going on?" he said.
"You know what you should do.
Don't cling on to Angry Clouds,
they'll make it worse for you."

"Say sorry to your sister,
for pushing her that way.
Then go and wash the dishes.
That's the price you have to pay."

He hated washing dishes,
more than anything at all.
He sneered up at the Angry Clouds,
then rain began to fall.

It fell so hard on Karma Kyle,
that he slipped right down below.
He landed in a puddle of mud.
He was drenched from head to toe.

When Shimi played her trunk,
in a very happy tone.
He said with an angry frown,
"Just leave me here alone!"

He fell into a deep, dark hole,
and bumped into a tree.
Angry clouds were with him.
He was angry as can be.

Bad Apple tried to trip him,
with a branch along his way.
Karma Kyle fell down to the ground.
His anger was here to stay.

Everywhere that Karma Kyle,
would even try to go.
Angry Clouds would follow him
and wave to say hello.

And on that gloomy day,
many people often said,
that Karma Kyle became so angry,
he turned from green to red.

His temper took a hold of him.
He roared and stamped his tail.
He even kicked Bad Apple,
straight into a garbage pail.

That was the final blow.
He could not take it anymore.
He looked up to the sky where
he could see Wise Owl soar.

16

"Oh there you are Wise Owl.
I'm so glad I found you here.
Angry Clouds won't let me be.
They will not disappear."

"Listen, listen Karma Kyle,
to what I have to say.
You can learn to make
those Angry Clouds just go away."

"Angry Clouds are like the weather.
They come and then they go.
Before they grab a hold of you,
don't let your anger grow."

"If you feel your anger now,
is growing big and tall.
Close your eyes and meditate.
It'll change from big to small."

"One breath in, one breath out.
That's what you need to try.
Good thoughts in, bad thoughts out.
Let Angry Clouds pass by."

18

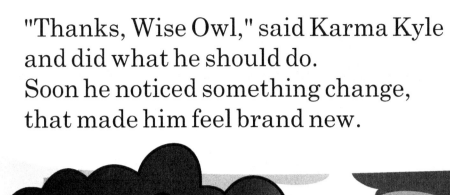

"Thanks, Wise Owl," said Karma Kyle
and did what he should do.
Soon he noticed something change,
that made him feel brand new.

When he opened up his eyes,
he looked up to the sky.
He watched the Angry Clouds
as they quickly passed him by.

Suddenly the sun came out.
It did not take so long.
All the colors had come back.
His anger had all gone.

On his way back home,
he stopped to go and play.
He saw his good friend Shimi,
and he wished her, "Happy Day."

"I'm sorry," said Karma Kyle.
"There was nothing I could do."
"I can understand," she said.
"Those clouds took hold of you."

And even when Bad Apple,
who made him trip and fall,
rode on Karma Kyle's tail.
He didn't mind at all.

He did not turn to red this time.
He did not stamp his tail.
He did not kick Bad Apple,
straight into a garbage pail.

He fell into the deep, dark hole
and bumped into that tree,
but nothing made him angry.
He was calm as you can be.

This time he did not push,
and things were not the worst.
He even let his sister go
into the bathroom first.

Karma Kyle did gladly,
what he hated most of all.
He cleaned up all the dishes,
every last one of them all.

The Karma Crocodiles,
would always try and sit.
Every night and meditate,
to calm themselves a bit.

Karma Kyle now realized,
you need to calm your mind.
So Angry Clouds don't have a chance
to grab you from behind.

Then Kacy threw a ball at him,
that hit him in the head.
He started to get angry,
but he did what Wise Owl said:

Angry clouds are like the weather.
They come and then they go.
Before they grab a hold of you,
don't let your anger grow.

One breath in, one breath out.
That's what you need to try.
Good thoughts in, bad thoughts out.
Let Angry Clouds pass by.

.....and they did!

The End

**KARMA KYLE
PRODUCTIONS**

Books that entertain themes of peace, calmness,
balance and moral responsibility to reinforce positive
emotions and behavior in young children.

CPSIA information can be obtained
at www.ICGtesting.com
Printed in the USA
LVOW02s1625280716

497658LV00001B/1/P